THE
CARSICK ZEBRA
and
Other Animal Riddles

THE
CARSICK ZEBRA
and
Other Animal Riddles

David A. Adler

illustrated by
Tomie dePaola

Holiday House / New York

To my good friend, Steven Blitz

Text copyright © 1983 by David A. Adler
Illustrations copyright © 1983 by Tomie dePaola
All rights reserved
Printed in the United States of America

Library of Congress Cataloging in Publication Data
Adler, David A.
    The carsick zebra and other animal riddles.

    Summary: A collection of animal riddles such as
"What dogs make the best librarians? Hush puppies."
    1. Riddles, Juvenile.   2. Animals—Anecdotes,
facetiae, satire, etc.   [1. Riddles.   2. Animals—Wit
and humor]   I. De Paola, Tomie, ill.   II. Title.
PN6371.5.A32   1983   818'.5402   82-48750
ISBN 0-8234-0479-X

Which dogs make the best librarians?

Hush puppies.

What would you call a frog that's stuck in the mud?

Unhoppy.

Why should you wear boots in a pet store?

You might step in a poodle.

What do you get from a mixed-up hen?

Scrambled eggs.

How do you get fur from a lion?

Run.

Which animal goes "cluck, bubble, cluck, bubble, cluck, bubble"?

A chicken of the sea.

How do turtles keep warm?

They wear people-neck sweaters.

How much does it cost to have a hippo's tooth pulled?

Twenty dollars for the tooth and $500 for the chair.

How do you lift a heavy duck?

With a quacker jack.

What did the judge say when five skunks walked into his courtroom?

"Odor in the court."

Which otters have heavy fur coats?

The hotter otters.

Which animal is black, white and green?

A carsick zebra.

What's big, gray and walks on one leg?

A hoppapotamus.

What do you get from a nervous cow?

Milkshakes.

What would you call a steamroller that runs over a goat?

A butter spreader.

Which animal is black, blue and green?

A bruised frog.

How do pigs keep from getting a suntan?

They wear oinkment.

What are Smokey and five of his friends?

A six-pack of bear.

What do you get when you cross a turkey with an octopus?

Enough drumsticks for Thanksgiving.

What's the hardest part about making hippo soup?

Stirring it.

What do cows read at the breakfast table?

The moospaper.

Which animals go "buzz, cluck, buzz, cluck, buzz, cluck"?

Electric chickens.

Why don't hippos play basketball?

They don't look good in shorts.

What stories do pigs tell their children?

Pig tales.

What weighs over a ton, has four legs and flies?

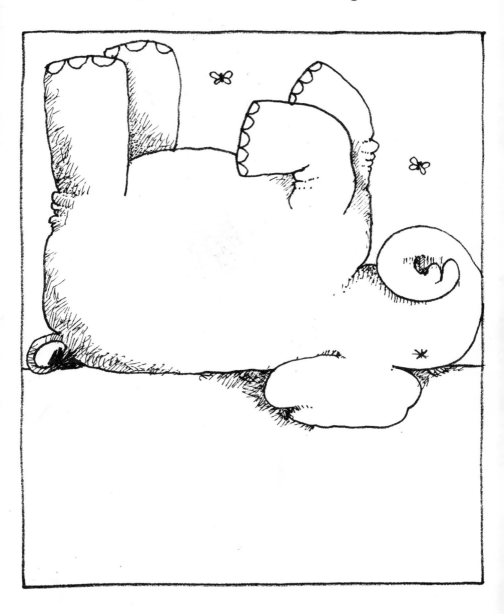

A dead elephant.

Did all the animals come on Noah's Ark in pairs?

No, the worms came in apples.

If ten lions were chasing you, what time would it be?

Ten after one.

Do you know how long cows should be milked?

The same as short cows.

What would you call a mosquito's pet rabbit?

A bug's bunny.

Which cat spends most of the day in the principal's office?

The cheetah.

How do you measure a snake?

In inches, because they have no feet.

What's gray, has four legs and a trunk?

A mouse on vacation.

What animal is black, white and red all over?

A zebra with measles.

Which animals are the best mathematicians?

Rabbits. They sure do multiply.

Who hides behind trees and scares campers?

Smokey the Boo.

**What did the teacher tell Gwen
when her pencil point broke?**

Get a pen, Gwen (penguin).

What has eight arms, wheels and a horn?

An octobus.

Who's fat, has a curly tail and WANTS YOU?

Oinkle Sam.

What's yellow and goes "putt, putt, putt"?

A golfing canary.

What do you get from pampered cows?

Spoiled milk.

When does a weatherman predict a feather storm?

When he sees a hen sitting on a bomb.

What has ten legs, black stripes and wings?

Two zebras and a canary.

Why is it hard to find a store that sells alligator shoes?

No one wants to wait on them.

What do you call a bee in a white sheet?

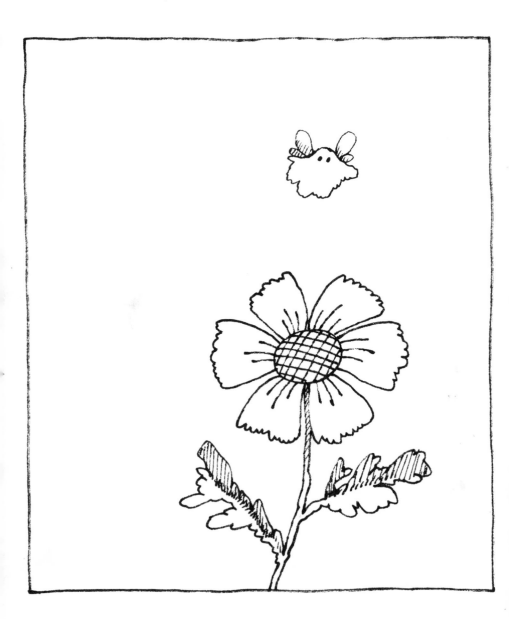

A boo bee.

What's fat, gray and has sixteen wheels?

A hippo on roller skates.

How can you tell the price of a pelican?

Look at the bill.

Which rabbits wear Band-Aids?

The ones with hare cuts.

How do you know that carrots are good for your eyes?

Because so few rabbits wear eyeglasses.

Why do ducks walk with their heads down?

So they don't quack up.

What did the parakeet say when his owner brought home a tiny bag of birdseed?

"Cheap! Cheap!"

What do you call a canary that flies into an electric fan?

Shredded tweet.

Why are elephant rides cheaper than pony rides?

Elephants work for peanuts.

What's green, fuzzy, and goes "quack quack"?

A moldy duck.

What do French frogs eat?

French flies.

Why do birds fly south in winter?

Because it's too far to walk.

Why shouldn't you bring a chicken to school?

It might use fowl language.

Why are restaurants so dangerous?

You might bump into a man eating chicken.

When do canaries have four eyes?

When there are two of them.

What did the chick say when she saw her mother sitting on a bowl of fruit?

Look at the orange marmalade.

What goes "buzz-a-choo, buzz-a-choo, buzz-a-choo"?

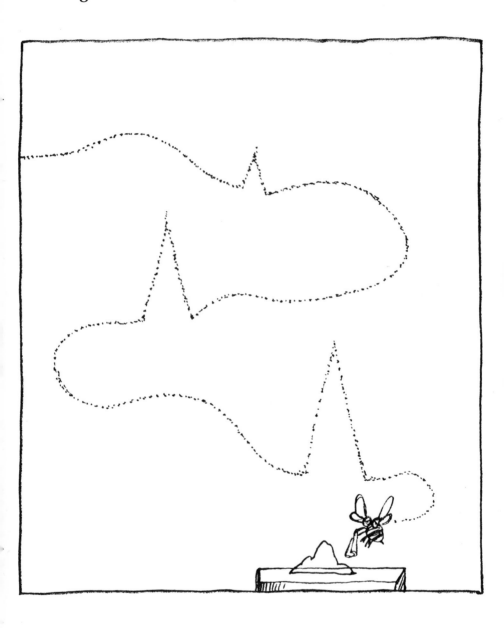

A bee with a cold.